The Bad Neighbor

The Ticket

This book contains two short stories and is a work of fiction. Names, places, characters, and situations are the products of the author's imagination. Any resemblance to actual persons, living or dead is purely coincidental. All characters portrayed in this book are 18 years of age, or older.

The Bad Neighbor

It all started about a month or so ago, my husband Sam and I had gotten married just before moving into our small apartment. Sam is twenty four and works for an insurance company. I'm only nineteen, and have been looking for a job since we moved in. Sam usually works long hours, trying hard to earn a good living for us. Some days, he doesn't make it home until late in the evening. He said that if he worked hard enough, they were bound to notice his potential and move him into a better paying position.

As newlyweds, we lived on the third floor of the apartment complex in a lower income part of town. It was the best we could afford just starting out like we were, and I was hesitant to move in. There were a lot of black people who lived in and around the apartment, and it was something I was not used to. I grew up in a rural community that consisted of mostly white people of European decent and I had never even had a conversation with a black person, let alone a friendship. All my preconceptions were based on TV shows and movies, and I found myself disdainful of their 'African' culture.

Since I still didn't have a job yet, I spent my days cleaning our apartment, doing laundry, and other various household chores. Unfortunately, our apartment did not come with a washer or dryer. Instead, our complex has a laundry room that's on the first floor. About two weeks ago, when Sam had gotten home, he said his company needed him to fly out of town to attend a business conference in another state. He really thought this was the opportunity we were waiting for. Sam busied himself by making us a nice dinner to celebrate, and so I hurried to finish the laundry.

Grabbing a basket of clothes, I left our apartment and headed toward the stairway at the end of the hall. About halfway down, I had to pass by a dodgy looking black man leaning against the wall talking on his cell phone. He was wearing those baggy pants that showed the top of his boxers and a hoodie. I tried not to look at him, but could tell he was checking me out. His eyes roamed over my body, and he had a sinister sneer at the corners of his goatee as he munched on a toothpick. I tried to ignore him, a shiver running up my spine. Casting my eyes down, I hurried past to the stairwell and down to the laundry room. After several minutes of loading laundry, I had forgotten about the stranger, and busied myself with starting the wash. Once the washer was loaded and running, I picked up my empty basket and headed back up the stairwell.

On the second floor landing, I rounded the corner and bumped square into the chest of the black stranger.

"Whoa there pretty thang", he said, holding my arms at the shoulder "what's your rush?" I stepped back a bit, startled by our run in.

"I'm sorry", I stammered, "I didn't see you there." The black thug smiled and looked me up and down, from my tight blue jeans to the plaid shirt I wore with the sleeves rolled up to the elbows, tied in a knot above my bare tummy. The top of my shirt was unbuttoned, giving him a good view of my ample cleavage. A skimpy lace bra, a gift from Sam, was clearly visible from his vantage point above me. My blond hair spilled down across my shoulders, and in front of my eyes. He took his hand off my shoulder and brushed the hair out of my eyes.

"I should really be going now", I said with a slight tremor in my voice.

"Not just yet", he said "You white bitches are all the same, scared of a brotha."

"I'm not scared" I said meekly, clearly terrified. I never really liked or trusted black people, they intimidated me. I was also not especially attracted to them either.

"Well miss uppity white girl, I got something you need to do for me first". He removed the basket from my hands and dropped it to the floor. Placing both his strong hands on my shoulders, he forced me down until I was kneeling on the floor in front of him. I knew I should have ran out of there, or screamed or something. I was hypnotized by this strange man and felt disoriented by his touch, unable to speak or move. He reached down and undid his zipper, sliding it all the way down. Reaching one hand deep into his pants, he pulled out the largest cock I had ever seen.

He waved his mahogany club mere inches from my startled face, my eyes wide with bewilderment. His fist gripped the base of his cock and at least six inches of angry black dick *still* protruded out from his hand. *Was this really happening?*

"Suck on it baby" he said, brushing the tip against my lips. Not seeming to be in control of my body, I parted my lips slightly and closed my eyes. The head of his dick pushed past my teeth, into my mouth and across my tongue. He placed his hands behind my head, knotting my hair into his fingers, and thrust deep into my mouth. The salty taste of his penis must have struck an involuntary nerve, and I closed my lips around his dick.

"That's it baby pull your lips across it". I don't know what came over me, but I reached up and gripped his shaft with both hands, stroking his cock as I licked and sucked his dick. He grunted and removed his hands from my head. Reaching down, he unbuttoned the rest of my shirt. Untying the knot at the bottom, he exposed my lacy bra completely. He then reached his hands around me and lifted up my shirt, quickly unhooking my bra. The bra fell to the floor at my knees, my breasts swinging free. His hands cupped my breasts, squeezing and flicking my nipples until they were hard.

"You are so hot baby" he said as he drove his cock deep into my mouth, causing me to gag. My ministrations on his cock sent him over the edge and he burst into my mouth. I tried to swallow as much as I could, but some of his seed managed to drip down between my bare breasts. He moaned and squeezed my breasts tighter and laughed. I felt ashamed and humiliated, swallowing hard. *How did I let this happen?*

The stranger released me and I stood up, grabbing my bra off the floor as I did so. He continued to chuckle as he put his semi limp penis back into his pants and zipped them closed.

"I'm going to fuck you tomorrow, so I want you to be ready for me." I couldn't believe this guy was telling me what he was going to do, and I didn't do or say anything, I just stood there looking meek as I put my bra back on and buttoned my shirt up over the stream of semen running down my chest.

"I want you to shave your twat bare, cause that's how I like it, and don't wear anything too complicated, if you catch my drift. I'll be at your apartment at noon, so be ready". With that he walked past me and gave my ass a quick swat. With a disdainful smirk on his face, he continued down to the first floor before disappearing out of the stairwell. I stood there for a minute dumbfounded, *did that really just happened? Did I really just let that happen?* I gathered my basket and straightened my clothes, wiping the excess sperm off my chin with a sleeve. I headed back to my apartment, not sure if I should or could tell Sam what had just happened. Would he understand that I was powerless? We finished our dinner, but I didn't eat much. I could still feel the stranger's semen churning in my stomach, the taste of his salty penis on my lips. I begged Sam to retrieve our clothes from the laundry room, feigning tiredness. I did not want to take a chance on running into the stranger again.

Early the next morning, Sam left for the airport before dawn. I didn't hear him leave and he left me sleeping in our bed. I was having second thoughts about keeping my secret. I needed to tell him what had happened and hoped he would understand that I was forced against my will. Because he left so early, I never got the chance. I vowed that I would tell him as soon as he returned.

I spent the morning getting myself ready to leave the apartment. I had no intention of letting some black savage into my home to fuck me.

While I was taking my bath, my thoughts drifted a million miles away. I had begun to shave my legs, and drifted to thinking of the black man in the stairwell. I remembered how he forced his will on me, making me suck his cock. Without realizing it, I had lathered my pussy with shaving cream and had unconsciously begun to shave it. I snapped out of my daydream, and discovered that I had shaved half of the pubic hairs from my pussy. I had to finish shaving the rest. I did not want it to look odd for Sam, so I continued to shave until my pussy was bare. I told myself that it definitely was NOT because the black stranger had told me to.

I finished my bath and dressed in a T-shirt and a pair of shorts. I paced the apartment as the clock drew closer and closer to noon, telling myself every minute that I was about to leave. *Why was I still here?* Finally, I decided that I would leave before the stranger had a chance to make his appearance. I grabbed my purse and keys and headed for the door. Swinging the door open I stepped out and ran directly into the black man from the day before. I gulped in air, shocked and surprised. I had waited so long to gather my courage to leave, that I didn't realize it was noon.

"Right on time", the stranger said, the sinister smirk still on his face. He pushed me back into my apartment and closed the door behind him, locking it in place.

"Wait, please, I don't want to do this" I said.

"Baby, you are so fine, before I'm through with you, you're gonna beg me not to stop." With that he guided me backwards toward the couch, sitting me down. He stood in front of me and removed his shirt, the hard muscles on his dark chest straining against his skin. I gulped, my eyes moving from him to the door, thinking I could make a run for it. He reached over and lifted my T-shirt up and over my head, casting it to the floor. His deft hands quickly unhooked my bra and my breasts bounced free. He placed his hands over my breasts and squeezed them lightly, flicking my nipples with his thumbs. It was then that I finally realized that it was inevitable, this strange black man was going to fuck me, and there was nothing I could do about it. I was not sure if I wanted to do anything about it.

He leaned me back into the couch and undid the buttons on my shorts. Gripping both my shorts and panties with his hands, he slid them over my ass and down my legs in one swift move, tossing them alongside my shirt on the floor. I was now completely naked and leaned back against the couch, my eyes glazed.

The black man looked down at my shaved pussy, and whistled.

"Oh baby, now that's what I'm talking about". He leaned over me, his hands roamed freely across my body, sending shivers tingling up my skin. I held my arms to my sides, gripping the couch cushions tightly as I turned my head away, ashamed and disgusted. Starting at my thighs, he worked his way up to my breasts. He dropped a hand down to my bare pussy and spread my labia, tweaking my clit with his fingers. I arched my back, and a gasp escaped my mouth. My pussy started to get wet from his manipulations, one hand rubbing deep while the other fondled my breasts. The black man stood back up and removed his pants as I lay there breathless from his fondling. Letting his large cock spring free, I had a flash back of him pumping it into my mouth, its salty taste spread across my lips.

He approached me on the couch and lifted my legs, placing them on either side of his bare waist. I could already see the pre-cum oozing from the tip of his massive hard cock. He pulled me forward until my ass was on the edge of the couch, my back flat against the cushions. He placed the head of his cock at the entrance to my pussy, and I could feel its head press up against my lips.

"Please", I begged one last time "I'm married". He didn't answer, and I lost my breath as the enormous cock split me in two, sliding roughly into my delicate pussy.

I screamed, the pain was intense and tears rolled down my cheeks. He pumped slowly at first, waiting for my pussy to accommodate his large girth. I couldn't speak and the pain was overwhelming, my hands flew to his chest as I tried to push him off. His cock stretched me to unimagined limits. My juices began to flow, finally lubing him up enough so he could glide in and out of me more smoothly. The pain lessened, and was replaced by pleasure I had never felt before. The tears on my cheeks turned to sweat as we perspired together. The hairs on his chest brushed against my hands and nipples with each of his thrusts and my legs quivered. I could feel the ridge on the head of his dick rubbing my insides, my tight pussy gripping his cock. My hands flew back to the cushions, fists clenching the material tight. My large tits would jiggle with every thrust. Just when I thought his cock was in me as far as it could, he hit a wall that gave some resistance, and then he sank in deeper. I couldn't talk or move, then sensations rippling through my body prevented everything but breathing.

Sam's dick was nowhere as big as this guy, and did not reach nearly as far into her as his now did. This muscular black stranger's cock had breached the place within her that no other cock, especially not Sam's, had hit before, striking virgin territory. I felt him hit the back of my pussy, poking my abdomen. I knew he was in me all the way when his balls started to slap the cheeks of my ass. His cock was so big, that my clitoris was forced down to rub the top of his shaft with every stroke. Even my hairless pussy was giving me sensations I had never felt before, as his pubic hairs rubbed the naked skin above my tender nub. I sensations were too intense, my body had never been filled this fully before and I exploded into orgasm, crying out as I came. My soft white legs sprung around his mahogany back, drawing him deeper into me as I threw my arms around his neck. My pussy clenched his cock ferociously, guttural sounds the only thing escaping my mouth. My juices ran freely down the crack of my ass and onto the couch as I felt him stiffen. He lurched into me as he erupted, his African seed spurting deep into my European-American pussy as he covered my mouth with his, his tongue wrestling with mine. He thrust a few more times, letting my convulsing pussy drain his semen before he collapsed onto me.

We lay there for a moment, letting our sweat mingle as his dick slowly began to shrink. I was overwhelmed with a desire for more, and guilt for having cheated on my husband, even if was unprovoked. The stranger could see the conflicting emotions on my face and pulled himself off of me.

"I want you to get onto the couch on all fours so I can take you from behind" he said. My heart lurched into my throat, but I obeyed and rolled over, placing my knees on the edge of the couch cushions, my elbows resting on the back of the couch. I looked back and could see that he was already getting hard again. A small thrill ran up my spine and I felt his cock part my labia again. He slid into me smoothly this time, and thrust slowly in and out.

His balls were hanging low, having drained most of his dark seed into me already, but his dick was as hard as ever. His balls smacked noisily into the backs of my thighs as be buried himself deep within me. He reached around and cupped my swaying breasts in his hands, tweaking my nipples and squeezing my soft mounds. I moaned as he laid his weight across my back, peppering my shoulders with brief kisses. His pace was smooth and steady, and I was quickly approaching another orgasm. But just then he stopped and pulled almost all the way out. He leaned up off my back and gripped my ivory hips, with his ebony hands, but he did not enter me again. He was toying with me, the tip of his dick the only part of him that was in me.

"Please", I said "fuck me, make me come. I'm your slave, your white slave and you are my black master. Take me master, punish me". I could not believe I was saying all this. It was only a short time ago that I was horrified at the thought of this black savage raping me, contemptuous of him and his race, and now I was begging him to fuck me, just like he said. I could tell that smirk had returned to his face again. I arched my back and tried to push back into him, but his hands holding my hips prevented them from moving. "Please" I said again, "fuck me, take me master".

He pushed quickly into me, and I gasped at the suddenness of it. His strong hands gripped the tender white flesh of my hips, my pussy clenching his monstrous tool. He pounded me hard now, and my hands lost their grip on the back of the couch. I fell forward, forcing my breasts to smash and flatten into the cushions, my arms dangling over the back of the couch. My breathing was getting harder, his cock stretching the walls of my pussy. He reached around and found my clit as his long black fingers strummed my pale nub. He rubbed it vigorously as his cock drilled deep within me, his fingers smearing the folds of my pussy as he squeezed my tender little bud.

Again, within a short period of time, my body erupted into a violent orgasm, my head held tight against the back of the couch. I was so young and innocent, so beautiful and vulnerable, that my submission to him brought him cascading to orgasm as well. Again he erupted into me, crying out in a loud grunt, the first time I heard him make a noise. His cock lurched inside me, soaking the walls of my pussy again with his seed. I could feel his semen squirt deeper within me than before, my pussy milking him once more until he was dry. This time, he collapsed onto my back, forcing me to flatten against the cushions, his cock buried deep within my bowels.

We lay there for a long time, breathing deeply. His rough dark hands massaged the soft light skin of my sides, from my hips to my breasts while leaving a trail of kisses with his wide lips across my face and neck. His big black cock would lurch every now and then as my pink pussy squeezed it reflexively, the last of my orgasm slowly fading.

Later, we showered together, and he fucked me again. We had sex several more times that day, and I loved every minute of it. He said he would be back, and was going to fuck me whenever he wanted to, as a true master should. Since then, he has made it a point to stop by whenever Sam is at work. We fuck for hours, and he has even fucked my ass several times. In a way, I have enjoyed the black stranger's unannounced visits. Letting him have his way with me, being his slave. But I also worry that Sam may find out. Now I have a new worry. Just yesterday I found out that I'm pregnant. I'm not sure if the baby is Sam's, or if it belongs to my black master who fucks me every day. I don't know what I'll say to Sam if the baby is black, but deep down, I know that it is. My master has shot his load deep into my pussy at least once a day, sometimes more, and I've only had sex with Sam a few times a week, and only if he is not too tired from work. I guess I'll have to wait and see. Poor Sam, he spends all day working hard, only to have his wife dominated and probably impregnated by a black man while he toils. But that will have to wait until my next story.

The Ticket

Driving home one evening from a party with friends, I never thought that I would end up handcuffed, riding in the back of a police car. But that's exactly where I was. I left the party early, dumped by my boyfriend and in tears.

I hadn't seen that red light, and blew through the intersection before I knew what happened. Luckily, the roads were deserted, but before I knew what happened, there was a police car behind me, lights a blazing.

I pulled over and wiped the tears from my eyes, upset at having been dumped and now probably with a ticket I would have to pay. I already had four points, and if I got another ticket, they would suspend my license. I watched the rearview mirror as a tall dark shape approached the side of my car. I rolled my window down just as a hulking policeman leaned in. He must have been six feet tall and rippled with muscle, his Smokey Bear hat inches from my face.

"You know why I stopped you ma'am?" The policeman said in a deep voice. I could see his eyes move down to the 'V' of my blouse, toward the red lace bra that peeked slightly above the neckline.

"I'm sorry officer, I didn't see that light", I pled.

"I'll need to see your driver's license and insurance please" he said as he brought his ticket book up to the window. Tears began to roll down my cheeks.

"Please officer, if I get another ticket they'll suspend my license."

"I'm sorry ma'am, that's the law" was his only reply. My hands shook as I fumbled for my license in my purse.

"Isn't there anything I can do? I would do anything to keep from getting a ticket, please?"

The officer hesitated for a moment, as if he were thinking, and then stepped away from my door.

"Go ahead and step out ma'am". I paused, not knowing what this officer wanted from me next, and then slowly unhooked my seat belt. Swinging the door slowly open, I placed my feet on the ground and stepped out of the car.

The cop was an imposing figure, his huge biceps laced with veins, a menacing gun strapped to his waist. I looked like a small doll next to this monster.

The night air felt cool on my bare legs, It had been warmer that evening when I left for the party, and had worn a pair of shorts and a pink blouse. My long blond hair fluttered in the slight breeze. My tears were now running freely down my face.

"I'm really sorry, officer" my voice barely above a whisper "What do I need to do? I'll do anything you tell me to do." The officer looked intently at me, and I began to shake. His voice was low ringing in my ears.

"I think you need to learn a lesson here," he said.

"Yes sir, I understand," I nodded slowly, but didn't know what he had in mind.

"Turn around slowly," the officer said, and I did, sure he was watching every move that I made. "Put your hands behind your back." Slowly, I reached behind my back, not certain if I was making the right decision or not. But the reality was that I seemed helpless to make any other choice. He placed a strong hand over mine, clenching the fingers of my hands together. I heard the faint click of the handcuffs when the cold metal bit into my wrist, first one hand, and then the other. He ran a finger up my bare shoulder, tracing a line from my elbow to my neck, and goose bumps broke out, skittering across my skin. He stopped at my neck and brushed my strawberry blond hair away from my ear. I could feel the hard muscles of his stomach when he leaned in and pressed against my hands locked behind my back.

"You've been a bad girl" he whispered into my ear. I was mesmerized by his breath against my creamy shoulder.

He guided me from behind, walking stoically toward the patrol car. The police officer opened the backdoor to his cruiser, and I was not sure what would happen next. I was handcuffed and helpless, terrified of losing my license or worse, going to jail.

I stopped at the door and he put his hand on my head, pushing me forward and into the back seat. Terror filled my mind. *Was he really arresting me?* Perhaps he was taking me to jail, but that didn't make any sense. Not for running a red light. He closed the door and got into the front seat. We were separated by a shatterproof clear divider, used to prevent criminals from attacking the police officer who drove the car. I looked out the side window at my car as we sped past it into the darkness. Oh please oh please don't let him take me to jail I said to myself as my car vanished into the night.

He drove in silence for a time, but I could see him look at me every now and then through the rear view mirror, a mischievous and sinister look in his eyes. How would I explain this to my father? I was arrested for running a red light? I heard him speak something into his car radio, but could not make out what was said. He then turned the car off the main road and drove onto a narrow gravel lane. *What the hell? This can't be the way to the police station.*

The car drove through an old chain link gate that stood open and sagging with age. He pulled the vehicle up to the front of an old abandoned building. It looked like this place had been deserted for some time, but had once been a busy factory.

The officer turned his car off and got out. He opened the back door and grabbed me roughly by the arm, jerking me from the car.

"What is this place, why did you bring me here?" I said, my voice trembling with apprehension.

"Just want to make sure we have a little privacy, we wouldn't want to be interrupted." He led me by the arms through the old front doors of the building and down a narrow corridor, his flashlight leading the way. I was terrified. What if this guy was some deranged serial killer?

We entered a dark room at the end of the hallway. He held my arm at the elbow in his strong hand, bringing me to a stop. I heard him feel the walls with his other hand, looking for the light switch. He found it and turned the lights on. The overhead lights were dim, but enough to make out the inside of the room. There were tables and chairs scattered about, and in places chains hung from the ceiling. This used to be a workshop of sorts, and a lot of the old equipment was still here. Dust and old paper littered the floor, and in several places, water dripped from the ceiling, giving the room a dank, damp smell.

He guided me toward one of the longer, wooden tables, turning me around to face him, placing my back to the table. He pushed me up against the table, the bottom of my ass just meeting the top of the table. I was not sure this was what I had in mind, and was having serious second thoughts about this whole situation. But his next movements confirmed that I was not wrong about his original intent. Strong hands went to my waist and pushed me on the table, onto my back, my arms trapped under my body.

"Lay still" he said, and disappeared under the table. *What the hell was he doing now?* I felt the wood under my hands move, startled at the unexpectedness of it. A small hole had opened on the table under my hands, and I felt him grip the handcuffs through it. I heard the faint click of metal as something was attached to the short chain between the cuffs. He crawled out from under the table, and I gave the cuffs a little tug. To my surprise, the handcuffs were hooked onto something under the table, preventing me from rising up.

He stepped back and started at me for a moment, amused at the dumbfounded look on my face.

"Please," I said, "We don't have to do this".

"Don't worry girl, you don't want that ticket instead do you?" I shook my head no, and he unhooked his police belt, placing it on the floor to his side. He then moved to the edge of the table between my legs. I could see the arousal in his face as his strong hands moved to my waist and unbuttoned my shorts. He slid the zipper down and yanked the shorts off my legs, leaving me bare from the waist down, with nothing but a thin red thong to cover my nakedness. I sucked in air at the swiftness of his determination. He gripped my thong on either side of my waist and pulled it down my legs. I was now nude from the waist down, my ass on the edge of the wooden bench, legs dangling in the air below it.

He hissed through his teeth when he saw my bare pussy. I always kept my pussy shaved and smooth, and I now knew this was something that turned him on. He moved forward again between my legs, and I could feel the bulge of his cock rub my private area through his trousers. He grabbed my left ankle, and raised it to the table, placing the heel on the edge. He pulled something from below the table and I could feel him secure it around my ankle. He then moved to my right ankle and did the same. I felt my pussy lips part slightly when he spread my legs, moisture beginning to glisten on the lips. When he released my ankles from his hands, I realized that I could not move my feet. They were tied somehow in place, leaving me completely immobile and vulnerable on the table.

He stepped back to admire the sight. I looked down between my breasts and watched him through the 'V' of my spread knees as he removed his shirt. My heart beat faster, my breath quickening. His muscles were huge, bulging as he reached down and undid his pants. In a moment, he was standing in front of me in nothing but his underwear. An impossibly huge bulge in his pants caused the elastic waistband to sit several inches off his waist. He was big, but I hoped that he would not be so big that it hurt.

He stepped between my legs again, running his hands over my thighs, massaging the skin. He started at my knees and worked his way up toward my waist. His tender ministrations helped me relax, and the ever increasing proximity of his hands toward my pussy made me wet. I could feel the juice from my pussy leak down the crack of my ass and onto the table.

He leaned in, his hard cock brushing against the outer lips of my pussy through the thin material of his underwear. I sucked a quick breath in at the sensation, wanting his big cock inside me. His hands made their way slowly toward my stomach, stopping at the bottom button of my blouse. He quickly undid the bottom button and worked his way up, undoing each button in turn, slowly exposing my chest and red lace bra. He undid the last button, opening the shirt up all the way and let it lay on either side of me. He let out a low rumble in his chest, pleased at the size of my natural features. He cupped my breasts through the fabric his with big hands, squeezing the mounds, feeling my nipples harden through my bra.

I moaned and felt his cock jump against my pussy. He was even more turned on than I was. There was no catch at the front of my bra, and he couldn't remove it without tearing it.

"Sorry babe, but this has to go," he said. I nodded, eyes glazed over with desire.

"Do to me whatever you want." I could see the eager look and excitement in his eyes at my words. His powerful hands gripped the material of the bra between my breasts and pulled away from each other. The fragile fabric tore easily, causing my ample breasts to jiggle free. He quickly covered them with his hands, kneading the firm orbs while his thumbs flicked my hardened nipples. I was now completely naked, tied down on the table at an abandoned warehouse with a strange man fondling my chest, and I loved it.

Forcing himself to gain control, he released my breasts and stepped back away from me again.

"There is something I gotta do first" he said and dropped to his knees. All I could see from my vantage point between my breasts was the top of his head. It was then that I felt his warm breath against my pussy lips, and I knew he was about to devour my most secretive area.

His rough tongue slowly split my lips apart, moving upward toward my clit.

"Oh, yes," I moaned, rolling my head to the left. He reached my clit and closed his mouth around it, sucking it gently. Lightning shot through me as I bucked my hips and I cried out. He pushed his tongue deep, tasting the sweetness of my pussy while his nose rubbed my swollen bud. The rough whiskers on his face teased the sensitive flesh of my inner thighs. He moved his arm around my leg, placing his hand on my abdomen. His thumb flicked my clit faster and faster. His tongue licked a long line from my anus to my clit, and before I knew what happened, I had my first explosive orgasm of the evening, I arched my back uncontrollably, my body breaking out into a flushed sweat, my tits bouncing up and down. But he didn't stop, drinking in the juices that flowed from my pussy. He placed soft kisses around my labia, spreading my juices across his face. I slumped back against the table, out of breath but wanting more. After being eaten out in such a manner, I need his hard dick inside of me.

He stood up and removed his underwear. His large cock pointed straight at my hidden chamber. He moved in closer, and rested his massive club against my pussy lips, the tip of his cock high over my belly.

"Just relax honey," he groaned. "I'm going to fuck you deep and hard." I mewed as he glided his cock across my pussy lips, his massive shaft rubbing my clit as he soaked it in my juices. He placed his hands on either side of waist and slid them softly up my sides, back to my breasts. He leaned in and captured a stiff nipple in his mouth, suckling my breast. I closed my eyes, lost in the sensation. He teased me like this for what seemed like an eternity, switching from breast to breast while this cock slid over my pussy lips.

Finally, he sat up, and I felt the tip of his cock at the entrance to my pussy. He placed his hands on my waist, and pushed slightly. His massive head split my lips and spread me open as he sank an inch into me slowly. I gasped, knowing how much was left. With unexpected gentleness, he took his time, slowly opening me up an inch at a time. I had never had this much cock in me before, and he was hitting places that no one ever had. My pussy clenched his hard cock as he sat motionless for a moment, giving me time to adjust to his size. I groaned, breathing heavy, my hands clenching at air, locked below the table.

He pulled out, leaving only the head encased in my cunt before pushing back in again, this time with a little more force. I felt every vein and bump on his cock as he slid back in, stretching my pussy impossibly wide. I could not be certain, but it felt like he went deeper than last time, brushing the deepest recesses of my pussy. My god, I thought, he wasn't even completely in me yet.

He pace quickened as my pussy loosened at his ministrations. He pumped furiously, and really began to fuck me hard. He thrust harder and faster, his strokes almost frantic, his pelvis slapping hard against my thighs as his dick split my well worked pussy wider with every stroke, his cock sinking to incredible depths. I could feel his balls as they slapped against my ass at the end of the table. His every stroke caused my body to lurch. He leaned into me and his mouth covered mine, his tongue probing deep, locked with mine. I could feel the hair on his massive chest as he pressed against my breasts. He brought his arms up laid them along either side of me, cupping my head with his hands as he continued to devour my face with his mouth. His cock continued to slide in and out. It must have been 12 inches long and at least several inches thick. My shaved bare pussy was being brutalized by his relentless assault, and I loved every minute of it. He tensed, his pace quickening, and I knew he was about to cum.

I felt a moment of panic through the fog that enveloped me, but the words caught in my throat. I never wanted this man to cum inside me, and he wasn't wearing a condom, but there was also nothing I could do or say in time to prevent it. It took only a second before I began to scream and writhe against him in a way I had never done before. My body felt hot all over, filled with electricity that I could have never imagined possible. My intense orgasm felt like the world was exploding and nothing on earth mattered except for the feelings coursing through my body. Suddenly, he erupted deep inside me as well, filling my deepest crevices with shots of his hot seed. He continued to thrust forward, lost in the embrace of a powerful orgasm and collapsed fully onto my chest, pushing the air from my lungs. He continued to thrust in and out of me, pumping what seemed like gallons of his sperm. My body did not seem to object, as my pussy, against my will, clenched and massaged his cock of as much as it could.

We lay together like that, locked in a sexual embrace, his cock buried deep within me, for a long time. Our sweat mingled together as we lay there, panting for breath, his strong hands stroking my face, my soft breasts pushed tightly into his hard chest. I felt his cock soften somewhat, but he still gave a slight thrust every now and then, causing my body to jerk under him slightly.

Finally, he raised himself off of me, letting his cock slide out of my passage, a feeling of emptiness remaining. He put on his underwear and pants and was looking for his shirt.

"Hey, what about me?" I said, confused. He tucked in his shirt as he turned toward me.

"Oh, you're not done yet, my buddies here haven't had their turn yet." Shocked, I looked toward the door to see two more cops standing there, grinning and rubbing their crotches. They must have come in while I was being ravished, and did not notice them.

"We never talked about me fucking anyone but you" I said, fear creeping into my voice.

"We never talked about fucking at all" was his reply. "You just assumed it was going to be only me. It's time to pay your ticket."

With that, he grabbed his gun belt and walked out the door. The other two cops, although not as big as the last one, were still pretty impressive. They leaned against the wall with broad smiles on their faces.

I lurched and struggled against the bonds that held me, unable to do anything more than shake a little. I tried for several moments to free myself, but stopped when I realized I was giving the cops a show, my breasts jiggling back and forth as I struggled.

One of the two cops were shorter than the other, but not really that short, he must have still stood at least six feet tall, the other one slightly taller, probably six foot two. The cops moved away from the wall and came towards me. The shorter of the two ducked under the table while the other positioned himself between my legs. I felt the click of a lever, and my handcuffs were freed from the hole. The cop between my legs grabbed my arms at the shoulder and heaved me up. My legs were still strapped to the table, but that worked to his advantage. He forced me up and over his right shoulder, my hands still cuffed behind my back. My stomach came to rest on his shoulder, the underside of my breasts brushing against the back of his jacket. He held me in place, one arm around my ass the other holding the backs of my legs, and waited while his partner undid the straps holding my feet in place.

Once free, the cop carried me away from the table like a sack of potatoes, oblivious to my cries of protest. I sobbed.

The cop lowered me to the ground, placing me on my feet, turning me away from him.

"Listen guys, I really need to leave. This was fun and all, but I can't stay here any longer" I pled. As answer to my protest, a strong hand gripped my jaw, forcing my mouth open. A large red ball and gag was placed in my mouth, the straps tightened securely behind my head. My blond hair, already matted with sweat, was now pressed tightly against the side of my face. Something wet dripped on me from above and ran down my back, my shirt and bra fragments lay tangled around my shoulders. The shorter cop stood in front of me and placed his hands on my hips, holding me in place while the cop behind me began to undo the handcuffs. At least I wouldn't be tied anymore, I thought.

The cop released one hand cuff, holding my arms in place with strong hands, and removed my shirt. The bra fell to the floor on its own, having already been torn. He passed my free arm to the cop in front, who took it and lifted it high above my head. What I hadn't seen yet, was the wrist restraints hanging from the ceiling. My free arm was quickly secured above my head, forcing me to stand on the tip of my toes. The cop behind me removed the handcuffs from my other wrist, and raised my other arm to another wrist restraint above my head. I muffled a protest through the ball gage as that arm was also secured to the ceiling, causing my breasts to flatten slightly against my chest. Both cops stepped away, admiring my perfect ass and body.

They still hadn't said a word yet, but began to undress. Another drop of water fell on me from above, landing on my chest, and running down between my breasts toward my belly. I looked up, but could not see where it came from in the gloom.

Once completely nude, I could see their large cocks dangling between their legs. *My God*, I thought to myself, *they aren't even hard yet and they have got to be at least seven inches.* The curly patch of hair above their cocks blended into the darkness of the room. Unable to voice my protests, I pled at them with my eyes. Both had strong chiseled features, and ripped abs. I could see their large balls hanging free behind their cocks whenever they moved, swaying back and forth. Masculine pheromones emanated from them. The taller cop, the one who carried me from the table, stepped to the wall at my side and pulled a metal lever. From somewhere above me, water began sprinkling down, soaking my body in a warm, wet fluid.

"Need to clean you up a bit" the shorter of the two finally said. With the water continuing to sprinkle down on me like a shower, both cops moved in toward me.

There must have been something mixed in with the water, because soap bubbles had begun to form near a drain in the ground. The two cops took up position on either side of me, the water raining down on all of us. The taller cop placed a hand over my left breast, hefting its solid weight in his hands, squeezing gently. He began to rub his hand over my breast, his other hand doing the same across my ass. The warm water across my skin was slippery and began to foam. The other cop, in position on my other side, did the same. They alternated between my stomach and breasts, rubbing their fingers across my flesh, washing the sweat of sex off of me. Their hands explored my back and ass also, gripping and squeezing me all over. The oily water allowed them to glide their hands over my skin in an extremely sensual way, arousing me despite my reluctance. I lay my head back and closed my eyes, lost in the warm embrace of their probing hands, letting the warm water run down my face and neck. I could feel their cocks occasionally brush against my outer thighs, the heaviness of them making me jolt with each passing thump on my thigh.

A hand moved down my back to the crack of my ass, fingers gliding between my cushions, rubbing the soapy water between my cheeks. Another passed over my lower abdomen, millimeters from the edge of my clitoris. I closed my eyes, sucking in air around the gag. The hand moved lower, teasing the lips of my pussy. Two fingers of the hand lay on either side of my lips. A third finger in the middle parted my lips and rubbed up and down. I moaned, unable to move away from the hand, held in place by the bonds and strong, probing hands. The fingers exploring my ass found my rectum and I jumped. The finger paused there, rubbing my anus, the palm of the hand squeezing my cheek. I felt a finger enter my pussy and my legs began to shake as I strained on my toes. The finger explored my hole, pressing deep into me. I ground my clitoris into the palm of the hand and tried to sink deeper onto the slippery finger in my pussy. That's when I felt the finger massaging my anus pause and push in slightly. When I tried to open my eyes, I couldn't. The soapy water made them sting, forcing me to keep them tightly closed. The finger in my ass was working its way in slowly with the help of the soapy water. I clenched my cheeks, trying desperately to prevent this unwanted intrusion. My anus betrayed me and opened slightly, allowing the finger to slip a little further inside. The finger twisted back and forth, loosening my muscles while the finger in my pussy continued to work its way in and out of me.

I could feel his knuckles in my anus as each segment passed through my rim, finally buried in me as far as it could go. The finger then began to pump in and out of my ass slowly, the double penetration of fingers taking my breath away.

Suddenly, the fingers withdrew from both my pussy and ass. I could hear the cops moving around me, but I still could not open my eyes. Two strong hands grabbed the back of my thighs and lifted my legs off the floor, my wrists taking the weight of my body. I felt my legs placed on either side of one of the cop's hips, and a heavy dick landed over my pussy. Breathing heavily, I felt the cock stroke slowly up and down over the outside of my lips, his balls pressed into the back of my thighs at the end of each upward stroke. He pulled back, and I felt the tip of his cock slide down to my entrance. We were both lubed up from the soapy water, and his cock slid easily past my lips into my cunt. I groaned as his cock filled my womb. He immediately took up a steady rhythm as he held my legs over his forearms, his hands gripping my hips.

I felt a muscular chest against my back, holding me in place while the other continued to fuck my pussy. Two hands lifted my ass and spread my cheeks. I felt a strong cock placed between the soft cushions of my ass, rubbing the soapy water through my crack. I gasped, my mouth opening even further around the gag as the cock pressed against my anus. The head of his cock stretch my anus open as the cock in my pussy continued its relentless thrusts. He continued to slide his enormous cock into me inch by inch in one slow penetration, eliciting a silent scream from my immobile form. I now had two large cocks in me, spreading both my holes to unimagined limits. The cop behind me reached around and cupped my breasts, massaging the soapy water into my hard nipples. In front, the other cop pounded in an out of me, the slurp of water around our sex highlighting the intense feelings coursing through my body.

Eventually, the sprinkle of warm water slowed and stopped. Apparently, it was timed to last for only several minutes. With the water no longer falling on me, I was able to pry my eyes open and look down. Still dizzy from the simultaneous reaming of my ass and pussy, I watched as the large cock glided in an out of my tender cunt, my legs held in place around the cop's waist by his strong arms. My hairless pussy was swollen and red, the nub of my clit sticking far out from its thin sheath of skin. I felt the cop tense and drive his cock deep and hard into me, using his hands to pull me close. His cock jumped and he groaned, spilling his load into my pussy in several short spurts. He continued to pound hard as his cock lurched, spitting semen into me with every stroke. Finally, he stopped, leaving his cock inside me and leaned forward. The cop behind me dropped his hands from my breasts and placed them on my waist, as the one in front replaced those hands with his mouth, suckling my breasts with his lips.

The cock in my ass began to pick up the pace, jiggling my cheeks with each of his thrusts. He took his right hand off my waist, and reached around me, furiously stroking my clit. With one cock pumping my ass, the other still buried deep in my pussy, and his hand rubbing my clit like there was no tomorrow, I couldn't take it anymore. Arching my back, I erupted into an orgasm the likes of which I have never felt before. My pussy and ass clenched both cocks, my whole body shaking, tits bouncing, ass jiggling. I screamed as loud as I could through the gag as both cops pressed into me, squeezing me between them. I felt the cock in my ass explode, shooting its seed deep into my anal passage. I have never been taken by two men before, much less while being tied up, but the feeling was incredible. My pussy continued to milk both cocks for several minutes, slowly climbing down from my intense orgasm.

The cop behind me reached up and undid my wrists from the restraints. I immediately placed both arms over the strong shoulders of the cop in front of me. We all sank down to our sides on the ground together, leaving their cocks deep within me. We just remained there like that for what seemed like hours. Not moving, but just relaxing in the feel of each other's tight embrace. The steam of the warm water still rose from the floor, my breasts pressed firmly into this strange cop's chest, another strange cop's chest pressed tightly into my back, and two large cocks deep in my holes. Our bodies were slick with water and sweat.

Eventually, with their cocks growing soft, they let them slip out of me, semen spilling out of my openings. They dried themselves off with a couple of towels they brought along, tossing one to me when they were finished. I removed the gag from my mouth and stood up, using their damp towels to dry myself. By the time I finished, both were dressed and watching me, grinning. I found my clothes and quickly put them on.

"Come on babe, let's get you back to your car" said the taller cop.

Several minutes later, I was sitting behind the wheel of my car, speeding down the road, asking myself if that really just happened. I wondered about how many other women have fallen prey to the same trap, and I wondered if I would ever see any of those cops again. I'm just glad I didn't get a ticket.

If you enjoyed this tale, please be sure to pick up these other erotic titles by K.J. Burkhardt

- Blackmail & Bondage
- Caught in the Vampire's Embrace
- Slave to the Vampire's Embrace
- Teaching Cindy: An Erotic Tale
- Biker Bang: An Erotic Tale
- Taken by the Monsters: An Erotic Monster Tale
- Photo Shoot Orgy
- Taken by the Tentacle Monster: Part 1: Baby Breeding!

- Blackmail & Bondage

Mrs. Johnson is a 19 year old trophy wife of a successful 50 year old CEO. When she receives a ransom note in the mail one day demanding she follow the instructions or her husband will be killed, she has no choice but to obey. Taken captive when she follows the letters instruction, Mrs. Johnson is forced to endure the depravities of the blackmailers, all while bound and gagged in an abandoned building until her own desires match those of her captors.

- Caught in the Vampire's Embrace: Book 1 of The Vampire's Embrace series

Tom is a normal guy with normal problems, his breakup with Heather devastating. Before he can move on with his life, he is accosted by a mysterious woman in red and seduced against his will. What Tom doesn't realize is the woman is a vampire, a creature of the night who makes Tom her own. But Tom's love for Heather is strong and he defies his vampire lover to be with Heather.

- Slave of the Vampire's Embrace: Book 2 of The Vampire's Embrace series

With Heather now a vampire like them, they flee across the country to prevent others from learning their secrets.
What they don't know is there are other vampires in the world and Heather and Tom are but pups to them.
A master vampire captures and seduces young Heather, using her as bait to lure the others to his grasp. Can Tom resist the temptations of a beautiful elder vampire? Will his lust for another doom Lydia? I guess you'll have to find out for yourself as the story takes a dark turn.

- Teaching Cindy

The landlord's daughter seduces John, a fifty something year old retiree.

Can John restrain this fiery vixen despite his burning desire for her young flesh? Will her yearning to feel a man for the first time tarnish his convictions?

- Biker Bang

Shannon's breasts and palms were plastered against the driver's window of the old Buick. The man behind her held a tight grip on her hips as he thrust rhythmically inside, his shaft repeatedly stretching her open beyond belief, pushing deep, deeper than she had ever had anyone inside her. Her legs quivered. Her breasts left twin, slick trails of her sweat running down against the window as she moaned in ecstasy.

Phil sat in the passenger seat, transfixed on his wife's nipples as they flattened against the glass. His penis swelled in his pants as this stranger took his wife from behind, using her body.

What started out as a normal drive into the country to visit friends on a lazy Saturday afternoon had turned quite suddenly into a free for all of sex and lust. And his wife was enjoying the whole thing.

- Taken by the Monsters: An Erotic Monster Tale

Amy gets more than she bargains for when she escapes a sudden downpour by taking shelter in an abandoned building. What she doesn't realize is there are Monsters in this building who want nothing more than to plant their seed deep within her.

- Photo Shoot Orgy

Amber had decided to let her friend Rob take some racy pictures of her to send to her boyfriend. But after several glasses of wine, she ended up in the nude with a lusting friend fondling her gorgeous body, and more...

- Taken by the Tentacle Monster: Part 1: Baby Breeding!

Tammy is happy with her life and her job as a model. But when her adoptive parents sneak home an alien creature from a government lab, it's Tammy who pays the penalty. The creature's nefarious agenda to impregnate as many Earth women as possible, sets into motion a chain of events that will shake the world to its core. Will these tentacles of pleasure consume the Earth? I guess you'll have to read to find out.

2198575R00020

Printed in Great Britain
by Amazon.co.uk, Ltd.,
Marston Gate.